CHEQUERS
or
KITTY ALONE

Chequers padded softly past [*p.* 96]

CHEQUERS

or

KITTY ALONE

By

JOAN WANKLYN

FREDERICK WARNE & CO. LTD.

LONDON & NEW YORK

Printed in Great Britain

CONTENTS

ILLUSTRATIONS

CHEQUERS
or
KITTY ALONE

CHAPTER I

CHEQUERS GETS HIS NAME

Little specks of dust danced in the yellow strip of light that slanted in through the cobwebby window high up in the wall of the loft. A door banged somewhere and the wind blew a rustling, papery onion-skin across the dusty floorboards and into the square of sunlight.

Away in the corner where the old potato sacks lay sprawled in an untidy heap something black and white moved, peering round the edge of a screening packing-case. The light gleamed on a pair of wide, inquiring eyes, and a small head craned farther and farther forward; then, all at once, a small, fluffy, black-and-white body shot into sight.

The onion-skin was twiddling round and round now, making a fascinating scuffling noise, and the kitten knew he simply had to catch it. But somehow

3

those short, wobbly legs of his just wouldn't behave themselves, and the twiddling, golden-brown skin seemed miles away.

He lurched on doggedly, and after tripping over himself and bumping his nose a couple of times he found himself on the edge of the sunlight. Then he decided he was going to be very cunning, and he bunched himself up into an untidy, tousled little ball, his ears half back and his eyes narrowed. He wasn't going to go chasing all over the floor after that skin —oh, no, he'd wait till it came swaying gracefully towards him, and then he would pounce.

Here it came at last! The black tip of his tail twitched with excitement and he bunched his hind legs up under him; then, with a mighty effort, he sprang—or at least he thought he sprang, but things didn't turn out quite right.

He landed on his tummy and he bumped his nose again and, worst of all, when he hoisted himself on to his fore legs and looked round with wide, puzzled blue eyes, there was his quarry twiddling away

4

merrily on the other side of the sunlight. It really was too bad, and he felt utterly miserable.

He began to feel very much alone, too, and he opened his small pink mouth and squeaked forlornly.

The black tip of his tail twitched with excitement

He wanted his mother as he had never wanted her before—wanted to feel the roughness of her tongue smoothing his fur, to hear her deep contented purring and snuggle up against her, back in the warm nest she had made among the sacks.

All at once she was there, butting him with her nose to find out if he was safe, and chivvying him

5

across to the corner. It was good to be back home again, to jostle and shove against the soft, warm bodies of his brothers and his sister, and sniff the dry, musty smell of the sacks and know that he was safe.

All that day he was very good, but next morning he had forgotten that he had been frightened and he only remembered how exciting the big loft had been. There was such a lot he wanted to find out now he had started; it was all new to him, for only a few days ago his eyes had been shut tight and he had done everything by feel and smell—and instinct.

For nine days he had been blind, a wriggling, helpless little bundle, sleeping, drinking his mother's milk, mewing a little and then sleeping again. Even when his round, innocent, slatey-blue eyes had opened, he couldn't see properly; everything was dim and blurred, but gradually he began to know the difference between light and dark, and slowly, as the filmy haze cleared, things outside the nest began to look exciting.

Twice more he ventured out by himself, and then

he lured his two brothers and his sister out too. And what a time they had! They chased onion-skins, they played football with little round potatoes, they tied

Torn paper bags littered the floor

themselves into knots with old forgotten balls of twine, and by the time they had explored everywhere and investigated everything the loft looked as if a gale had swept round and round it. Torn paper bags littered the floor, the potatoes were mixed with the carrots, a pile of cardboard boxes had been tumbled

7

down, a sack of sawdust had burst, and the string festooned everything.

Then one day, in the middle of a wildly exciting game of tag—their mother was out mousing in the

The string festooned everything

yard—the piebald kitten suddenly skidded to a halt and stood stock-still, his head on one side and his absurdly large black-and-white ears alert and listening. His black brother couldn't stop himself and bumped into him, and it took a little while to sort themselves out. When the piebald kitten was on his

8

legs again, there was no doubt at all that very suspicious noises were coming from the direction of the ladder leading down to the stable.

He didn't like it at all. He waited a moment longer and then turned tail and fled for the nest, with the others helter-skelter behind him. There was a traffic jam at the narrow corner by the crate, but at last they were all safely hidden, listening to the heavy stump, stump on the ladder with hearts pounding against their small ribs.

Then something dark and tremendous appeared in the doorway—the piebald kitten saw it because he couldn't resist poking his head round at the last moment. There was a click and the whole place was lit up with a dazzling brightness that made the square of spring sunshine on the floor look pale and indistinct. He was too astonished to bob back out of sight, and before he knew what was happening the terrifying creature had picked him up by the scruff of his neck and was leaning over the crate staring down at the other three cowering behind it.

"Kittens, eh?" said the giant, who was Mr. Alfred Dingle, the greengrocer who owned the kittens' mother, the loft, the stable down below, and the little shop beside it. Then he turned round and looked at the litter all over the loft.

"Bless my soul!" he said, "the little rascals! What a pretty mess!" But being a kind-hearted man, he muttered something about having to clean it out anyhow, and, looking at the piebald kitten, he tickled him under the chin with one enormous finger.

"Just like a draughtboard," he chuckled. "H'm, yes, 'Chequers' is the name for you, my lad!"

But Chequers only drew back his small pink lips and hissed manfully, and when the finger came within reach again he nipped it with all his might.

"You little spitfire!" yelped Mr. Dingle, hastily dropping Chequers, who squeezed himself into the darkest corner and tried to pretend he wasn't there at all.

All at once there was a scamper of paws across the floorboards and their mother slipped round the packing-case and, after sniffing them all in turn, pushed her black nose into the greengrocer's huge hand, giving little purrs of pride as she showed off her family. Mr. Dingle forgave Chequers, and said what a clever old thing Blackie was to have hidden her nest so well. Then, after filling a sack with potatoes, he went thumping down the steps again, and Blackie started washing the kittens until all the man-smell was gone.

Down in the kitchen behind the little shop Mr. Dingle told his wife about Blackie's new family, and they wondered who would like the kittens when they grew older. Chequers ought to have felt proud, because he was the only one with a name, while the others were just "the Tabby One", "the Black One", or "the Mostly White One", but he was much too busy wondering just how he could get down those steps and find out what happened at the bottom.

CHAPTER II

BLACK MONDAY

Chequers didn't manage it until a week later, when he had grown another half-inch and felt he knew all there was to know about keeping his legs in order. He chose a time when his mother was away—she always sunned herself in the shop window for an hour or so in the mornings—and he made quite sure the other three were sound asleep, with eyes shut tight and little pink tongues peeping out of their mouths. He knew it was much too tricky a business to risk one of them cannoning into him and making him lose his balance.

He took one last look at them, and waddled solemnly across the floor. He felt very daring, and a tiny bit nervous, but just to show how cool and collected he was he strolled casually past the doorway the first time and pretended to sniff at something that didn't interest him in the least.

12

At last he stood looking down to the floor of the stable below. There was a champing and a stamping going on down there, but he had tried to find out

He lurched forward, scrabbled frantically, and felt himself falling

where it came from before, and he knew that however much he craned and stretched perilously over the brink he couldn't manage it. A fascinating, fragrant scent came wafting up to him, quite different from the earthy, rather fusty smell of the loft. It made him long to find out all about everything, but now he had come to the point it seemed a very long way down to the first step.

He sniffed over to the right to see if it looked better from there, but it didn't. He edged forward, digging his sharp little claws into the dry woodwork. Farther and farther he leaned—lurched forward, scrabbled frantically, and felt himself falling.

He landed with a thump on the step and picked himself up, feeling rather shaken. Still, now he had started the others didn't look so bad. Thumpety-bump, thumpety-bump, he went down and down, until, when he looked back, the doorway seemed endlessly far away. It was quite exhausting, so he sat down and gave himself a breather, and then started on the second stage.

At last he stood at the bottom and gazed all around him, hardly knowing which way to turn. There was a wide door to one side that led out into the yard, and another half-open one beside it, through which he heard Mr. Dingle's voice as he talked to customers. Behind him he heard the restless stamping and rustling again, and he cocked one ear back, still undecided. Then he turned and padded towards the noise, paused behind a jutting wall, and peered round stealthily.

Gertie, the pony, didn't stop her lazy munching, and Chequers grew bolder, but just as he was about to edge out from the wall Gertie chose to stamp her hind leg and shake her head so that her head-chain rattled in the most alarming manner.

Whenever Gertie moved, the straw she stood on rustled invitingly; Chequers was just longing to take a flying leap into it, but he hesitated, shifting his pads and working his claws in and out thoughtfully. Then, as nothing very terrible seemed to happen even when Gertie moved, he bounced forward, his tail held stiff for a couple of inches and then drooping absurdly. Gertie deigned to notice him for the first time and blew at him. He was a little taken aback, but it wasn't very awful really, so he dabbed experimentally at the straw.

15

It was better than he had expected and, forgetting all about Gertie, he bunched himself up and plunged into the middle of it. Gertie snorted and jerked her head up indignantly—really these young things had no idea of the respect due to her, an old lady of twenty-one! She'd show the impudent little thing!

She laid her ears back and raised one hind hoof threateningly. All the other kittens, puppies, and any other nuisances Gertie had known always fled at her danger signals—in fact, people called her a cross-patch, and she was rather proud of it—but this piebald object didn't take the slightest notice. It just went on rolling and scuffling and turning somersaults in the same ridiculous way, and now it had burrowed under the surface and come up clutching a wisp of straw, kicking and tearing savagely at it as if it was some fierce and dangerous animal.

Gertie didn't know what to do. The Object had rolled right under her, and she didn't dare to move in case she stepped on it; in fact it was a good two minutes before she managed to put the threatening

16

hind leg down. By that time Chequers was lying spreadeagled on his tummy getting his breath back. Then he sat up as if he was bored with the whole business and, seeing Gertie looking at him, pretended to be very coy. He couldn't blush, but he gazed down at the straw and patted it daintily, looking too good to be true. For a moment he stayed there, and then, in a flash he was up and away, careering round and round, in and out between the bewildered Gertie's hoofs—and the strange thing was that she didn't mind in the least; indeed, she was enjoying it all.

Suddenly Chequers decided he was tired and, plumping himself down where he stood, he was asleep in two seconds. His mother found him there, curled up in a dusty, rumpled ball after she had searched frantically all over the loft. Blackie didn't like Gertie, and the pony didn't like her, but Chequers obligingly solved the problem by waking up and dancing towards his mother—not in the least repentant for the trouble he had given her.

Then the fun started. He couldn't get back up to the loft.

However much his mother coaxed him and shoved him he just couldn't haul himself up those steps, and in the end Blackie had to move the whole household down to him, lifting the other reluctant kittens by the scruff of the neck and dropping them down on to the top step. Chequers was out of favour for the rest of the day.

It was wonderful being out of the loft and they all thoroughly enjoyed themselves—especially Chequers. Of course, he was the first to invade the shop and the kitchen—in fact, there was no telling what he would get up to. He explored among the piles of chips in the wood shed, all over Gertie's four-wheeled cart, and along her manger. It was while he was walking delicately along the top of the partition of her stall that he saw the nosebag. It was hanging from a nail in the beam, and it was deep and exciting-looking, and he couldn't see the bottom of it so, of course, he wanted to. He stretched his paw down into it as far

The nosebag was deep and exciting-looking

as he could reach, but it seemed to go on for ever. He leaned forward, wobbled a moment, and then it happened—he dived in head foremost!

19

Gertie rolled wide eyes round as the nosebag swayed and bulged, and muffled sneezes came from it when scraps of chaff tickled Chequers's nose. There was a frantic scrabbling as he tried to hook his claws on to the tough canvas, but it was no good; he was stuck.

He wasn't found till Mr. Dingle came to drive Gertie out to the market-garden to collect a load of greens and onions, and the poor man nearly had a fit when he saw a dancing nosebag.

But that was only the beginning of the scrapes. They happened so regularly that Chequers got a reputation. Instead of talking about the weather while Mr. Dingle weighed out the sprouts and sorted out the pennyworths of parsley, the customers asked, with a knowing chuckle, "What is the latest about that black-and-white scamp of yours?"

Mr. Dingle would mutter uncomplimentary things under his breath and recount the latest—how Chequers had fallen into the soap suds, upset the saucepan stand, or made dirty padmarks all over the best tablecloth.

Then Chequers would come strolling in and flop carelessly down across Mr. Dingle's shoes, gazing up out of appealing blue eyes and simply asking to be petted. And, of course, he was. Mr. Dingle forgot and forgave, and everybody said, "What a beautiful kitten!"

Chequers knew from the tone of their voices that they were talking about him, and he knew perfectly well that he was beautiful. He was beautiful and bad. That was the trouble.

One day—it happened to be a Monday—it reached a climax; things just happened one after the other. It started early in the morning when he dashed underneath the milkman's feet and made him drop two quart bottles. The rest of the kittens and even Blackie thought it was wonderful, and paddled happily, lapping right and left, but Mr. and Mrs. Dingle and the milkman didn't appreciate the joke.

Chequers retired to Gertie's stall while tempers cooled down. After a short rest he went mountaineering in the barn and managed to knock down a pile of flower-pots. Just before lunch his Mostly White brother decided that Chequers was getting too much lime-light and, when Mrs. Dingle's back was turned, he

He managed to knock down a pile of flower-pots

rolled all over the neat rows of carrots she had just sowed in the little garden behind the yard. Chequers, who happened to be near by, joined in and enjoyed himself so much that he didn't see Mostly White beating a hasty retreat, and he never realized that Mrs. Dingle was stalking him till it was just too late. Being beautiful didn't do him any good this time.

Feeling furious, Chequers crossed the garden with great dignity and sat sulking on the top of the wall, but he didn't stay still for long—the end of the washing line was flapping invitingly just above his head, swaying to and fro in the breeze, twisting itself round the post and playing hide-and-seek with him. He tore madly round and round after it, catching his claws in the knot at the end and swinging from it. He never noticed that the fastening at the head of the pole was working loose, but he did see the line sag in the middle until the washing almost touched the damp grass.

Chequers was learning caution, and he looked carefully round to see if anyone was looking. Then he hid behind the post, peeping round first one side and then the other as if the trailing table-cloths and towels were fearsome enemies.

He hunched himself up to spring, twitching his tail and setting his ears back, and just as the brightest bath towel dipped to the ground he pounced. He fought it savagely, biting, scratching, rolling himself up in it, tearing it with his hind feet. The line dipped perilously, there was a slither as the cord slid round the groove at the top of the post, and then the whole lot was down.

Chequers, almost smothered underneath a pair of pyjamas and another towel, wasn't at all sure what had happened, but he had a feeling that it was time he moved elsewhere. He squirmed and scuffled, half choked underneath muddy folds, and at last wormed his way out. Instinct made him pick himself up and bolt—but not before he had been seen.

"That settles it," said Mr. Dingle, after he had closed the shop that evening. "He's got to go."

Chapter III

NIGHT OUT

The Dingles had arranged where the other kittens were to go, but they had wanted to keep Chequers as a companion for Blackie. They talked it over solemnly, while in the barn Chequers slept in a curled-up bundle, with his tail tucked neatly round and his fore paws folded across it.

By the time supper was finished they had settled it all—Chequers was to go to Mr. Sprigge who kept the antique shop. Poor man, they said, the place was so overrun with mice that it would never do for him to be without a cat, and by himself Chequers would soon grow up and learn to behave. Mr. Sprigge had only just moved into the little low-fronted shop across the road, so he wouldn't know anything about Chequers's reputation, until the neighbours told him —still, that would take care of itself.

So in the morning, before taking down the shutters, Mr. Dingle called on Mr. Sprigge, who was delighted with the idea and thought it was "so kind and neighbourly". Mr. Dingle coughed and asked when he would like the kitten, and it was decided to bring Chequers over straight away. Mr. Sprigge chuckled happily and started pouring some milk into an antique saucer with a design of black kittens round the side, and he even put the butter ready to rub on Chequers's paws.

Mr. Dingle went back and unlocked the barn-door, opening it cautiously just a few inches so as to be sure Chequers wouldn't get out. Blackie and the three other kittens were there with their noses glued to the crack, but not a sign of the piebald. Unwarily Mr. Dingle opened the door a little wider, and in that moment Chequers was out and away. He had been skulking round the corner wondering if he were still in disgrace, and he thought it would be wiser not to wait to find out.

Chequers sat down in the middle of the yard and

26

watched Mr. Dingle lumbering towards him. It was strange that Mr. Dingle should want to catch him, and suddenly a little devil of mischief entered into him and he went dancing away, keeping just out of reach. The chase grew fast and furious, and Mr. Dingle grew hot and furious. At last Chequers climbed on to the steeply sloping roof and decided to get stuck. He had to be rescued with a ladder, and was carried over in triumph to Mr. Sprigge.

He didn't understand the butter-smearing ceremony at all, but he did understand the contents of the antique saucer. After he had finished up the last drop and had carefully licked his lips and wiped his whiskers, he investigated the shop and every hole and corner upstairs and downstairs, and he found it was good. He was just beginning to be interested in new and exciting smells, and the scent of mice was everywhere; it would be a good place to remember if he was bored at any time. Then he decided it was time to go home.

He was puzzled when Mr. Sprigge seemed to have

27

other ideas on the subject, but with a flirt of his tail he darted between that gentleman's spindly legs, scampered through the door, across the narrow pavement, and out into the street.

There was a terrifying screech from the right, and a huge shadow swung across him. There was another screech and a thud as a van bumped into the back of the lorry that had stopped first. On the other side a milk pony skidded to a halt and angry drivers honked their horns. Chequers sat back on his haunches with his mouth open in a defiant hiss, rooted to the spot with fright. Then he heard footsteps behind him and Mr. Sprigge's voice calling "Kitty, Kitty", and he found he could still move. He shot towards Mr. Dingle's doorway, through the shop and into the barn, where he found Blackie and the other three enjoying their breakfast. He shoved his way into the middle and, pretending he was starving, wolfed down far more than his fair share until his tummy was like a balloon.

When Mr. Sprigge came to fetch him he simply

hadn't the energy to move, and purred contentedly as he was carried back.

After a short nap on a cushion in an antique brass coal-scuttle he felt more himself, and when Mr. Sprigge was busy with a customer he sauntered out once more. The street was still rather a problem—he couldn't get used to things plunging towards him at such a speed, and a motor bicycle roared by within an inch of his tail as he fled the last few yards, but he recovered his dignity once he was safely on the other side.

This time he was clever. He didn't go in at the shop door. He squeezed underneath the yard gate and spent the next quarter of an hour cutting mad capers in the straw in Gertie's stall. No one was looking, except Gertie, so it didn't matter about dignity. Then he sprawled himself on a mat in the cart and slept again.

By the time he had gone backwards and forwards four times, Mr. Sprigge took it for granted that whenever Chequers disappeared he would be across the road. The fifth time it happened Mr. Sprigge had

29

A black-and-white tail drooped over the top of the coal-scuttle

just finished preparing the kitten's supper. Call as he would, no Chequers came, so off he went once more. He hunted high and low but still no sign of anything piebald, and despairingly he went home again—to find the supper saucer empty. Then it was that he saw a black-and-white tail tip drooping over the top of the coal-scuttle, and inside lay Chequers, the picture of innocence, with a "butter-wouldn't-melt-in-my-mouth" look on his face.

After a week Mr. Sprigge thought that it was time the kitten started earning his keep. Since Chequers insisted on having his days to himself and showed no sign of seriously investigating the mouse-holes, Mr. Sprigge decided to shut him up in the cellar for the night and see what happened.

Having been lured on to the rickety wooden stairs, Chequers heard the door bang behind him and found himself in the dark and alone. He didn't mind that, but he was furious at having been shut in. He poked his nose underneath the door at the head of the stairs and miaowed twice, but nothing happened. Chequers wasn't the sort of kitten to go on crying with no result, so he gave it up as a bad job and pattered down the steps to explore.

A pale, bluish light from a street-lamp outside came in through a dusty window looking out on to the area, and he saw that a pile of boxes and old furniture was stacked against the wall. He took a flying leap for a table-top and, balancing precariously on a pile of books, stood up on his hind legs and tested the boxes. There was a clatter and tinkle of broken pieces as a china bowl tipped off the top of the pile and the boxes wobbled, but Chequers decided he would risk it.

It was a hair-raising climb but he managed it, and by standing on tiptoe he could rest his paws on the window-sill, which was fairly broad. If he could reach the sill he could at least see out, which wouldn't be so bad, so he sat back and measured the jump. It was going to be tricky, because he would have to land sideways, but he thought he could manage it. He gave a last wriggle, tensed, and then thrust himself upwards with a terrific kick of his hind legs. He had judged it perfectly, and made a landing that even Blackie would have been proud of, but the jerk was too much for the top-heavy pile of junk that he had climbed. It swayed outwards, teetered, and then slowly and gracefully cascaded to the floor. The crash was awe-inspiring, but Chequers didn't care. Serve those interfering humans right!

The only trouble was that there was no way now of getting down, but he wouldn't bother about that till the time came. He stood up and looked at the window, pushing his nose against it and peering through the dust and grime. There was something sticking out from the glass just above his head, and he stretched up a paw to find out what it was. It crackled as he stuck his claws into it, and he found it was a scrunched-up ball of paper. This might be fun. He pulled experimentally, and the paper moved. When he pulled again it came away and went bouncing down to the floor, but suddenly he wasn't interested in it any more—he saw that a pane of glass was missing.

It wasn't easy hoisting himself through the pane, and once he nearly lost his balance. The ledge was narrow and sloping on the outside, and he never quite knew how he squirmed on to it, but there he was, and that was all that mattered. He took another breath-taking leap across to the side of the area, squeezed between the railings, and then he was free!

It was a wildly exciting night. He had never been out in the dark before—the Dingles' barn was his home and he had never wanted to escape from it—and the mysterious black shadows, the pale gleaming of the lamps and the eerie flitting moonlight were all new to him.

He listened to the serenading of a pair of cats along the street and he thought it was the most wonderful sound he had ever heard. Someone flung open a window and he heard the splash of water. The song ceased abruptly and he heard a pad-pad on the coping above him as the singers moved on to a quieter neighbourhood. He stared up and caught a glimpse of them hurrying by. What they could do, he could do too; so he clawed his way up to the top of a paling and then on to a low-jutting gable, and started climbing up the smooth, sloping tiles. There was nothing to get a grip on, but he knew it wouldn't do to get stuck as there was no Mr. Dingle to rescue him this time, so with much slithering and scraping of claws he managed it.

When he reached the ridge of the roof and looked round, panting, everything was so different that he was almost bewildered. Then he caught sight of the two serenaders prowling silently along a ridge, and he stalked them stealthily.

He played hide-and-seek with himself round chimney-pots, he bounced up and down gables, and he dashed wildly along narrow ledges until he was so weary that he hardly knew how to put one foot in front of the other. For a while he thought he was lost, and then, after a frantic hunt, he found Mr. Sprigge's back yard, slithered down the wall, and squeezed himself through the kitchen window. He was so sleepy he didn't even miss the Dingles' barn—he just crawled into the coal-scuttle and slept.

He woke just as the first sunlight was peering in through the chinks in the shutters and, after yawning and stretching and washing himself with his tongue, which was still too small, he decided he was hungry after all his exercise.

He lay quite still a moment, listening. Faint scuffling noises came from all around him, and for a moment he didn't know what they were. Then the instinct of his people told him what to do. He moved as he had never moved before—smoothly, tensely, like his mother when she was hunting. He eased himself out of the coal-scuttle and dropped to the floor with only the faintest thud. The scufflings stopped suddenly, and he lay still, scarcely breathing, his eyes watchful. Little by little the noises started again, and he turned his head from side to side, his ears working and his nose wrinkling until he knew just where they came from. Then he saw a small shape scuttle across a narrow band of sunlight, and in a flash he sprang, snapping his teeth together.

When Mr. Sprigge came sleepily down to get the breakfast on, Chequers was waiting for him, gently waving his tail and purring, and beside him on the

He solemnly watched the mystery of tin-opening

carpet lay a mouse—the third one—he had eaten the first two.

Mr. Sprigge made a great fuss of him, and Chequers swelled with pride. He pattered behind Mr. Sprigge to the larder, feeling in his bones that something good was coming, and solemnly watched the mystery of tin-opening, which he didn't understand at all—but he did understand the sardines when they came out!

Then Mr. Sprigge remembered that he had locked Chequers into the cellar—and he remembered too that just before he had gone to sleep he had heard the most amazing noises from down below.

He peered cautiously into the cellar from the head of the stairs, and it was much worse than he had expected. He shut the door hurriedly and looked down at Chequers who beamed up at him with an ecstatic expression and flopped against his legs.

"All right, old man," said Mr. Sprigge. "You win!"

CHAPTER IV

CHEQUERS GOES A-ROVING

The summer passed happily for Chequers, for Mr. Sprigge had learned wisdom and never interfered with him. Chequers did his duty, and the mice grew scarce, but during the day, and part of the night, he roamed.

When Black Brother, Tabby Sister, and Mostly White were given away, Chequers went to visit them, clambering over the roof-tops in the moonlight and enticing them out. He taught them what fun midnight climbs could be, and they were apt pupils. Then, sometimes, he went to keep Blackie company, and he always played in Gertie's stall and took a nap in her cart.

As the summer passed and the air had a frosty nip to it before dawn, Chequers lost his baby charm. He had grown, and his eyes had changed from blue to amber. He was never actually gawky like the other three, but he was definitely at the growing-up stage. His fur was long and silky—now his tongue was a

He kept his fur sleek and smooth

more respectable size he kept it sleek and smooth— and that saved him from being lean and angular. Although in public he behaved with great grown-up dignity, by himself or with his brothers and his sister, or at night, he was still a kitten—especially when he was playing in the straw.

40

He always seemed to be turning somersaults; he had started the trick accidentally when he was a kitten, but now he did somersaults for fun. He would make a lightning dash at something in the straw, then suddenly check in mid-gallop and go bowling over and over. He would sit up, pretend he couldn't understand what had happened, and then do it all over again.

One September morning he went through his routine as usual, and then retired to the cart to clean himself up, which was very necessary as he was covered with wisps of straw. When he had finished his toilet he strolled farther back into the cart and sniffed inside a case lying on the floorboards. There was a comfortable sack lying at the bottom and he hopped in, curled himself round till he was comfortable, and dropped off to sleep.

He didn't hear Mr. Dingle come into the barn, and he didn't hear Gertie being harnessed by Ned, the boy who drove the cart. He didn't know Ned was going to drive out to the orchard at Cross Roads

Farm, and he didn't see Mr. Dingle and Ned go across to a pile of crates and start carrying them across to the cart.

The first thing he heard was a crash just above him, and he sat up with a jerk, bumping his head on something hard. There certainly hadn't been anything on top of him when he had climbed into the box, but now it was as if a lid had clamped down, and he was shut in. He heard Mr. Dingle's voice talking to Ned, telling him how to find the Cross Roads, and he miaowed as loud as he could, but at that moment there was a second crash as Ned threw another crate on top of the pile.

Chequers miaowed again, but it was muffled by the box and the sacking, and still more cases were piled on top of his prison and on either side of it, stacked up as high as the tarpaulin roof of the cart.

Chequers was desperate. He couldn't bear being shut in, but there was no way out. He listened, with eyes wide and ears flat, as Gertie was led out of her stall and harnessed up, and then with a jolt the cart was moving.

They rattled out of the yard gate, and Ned urged Gertie on and she broke into a trot. The cart swayed and bumped, and Chequers had to brace himself against the side of the box to keep steady. It seemed ages before Gertie slowed down and then stopped, and Chequers felt he was bruised all over. He heard Ned's voice again and the farmer's, and he gave the loudest and most heart-rending miaow that he could invent.

"Did you 'ear something, Mr. Rogers?" said Ned, looking puzzled.

"Eh, what's that? Speak up, boy, speak up!" roared Mr. Rogers, who was just a little deaf.

"I said, did you 'ear something, sir!" Ned roared back in a mixture of bass and treble (his voice wasn't quite sure whether it was grown-up or not).

"Bless my soul, impudent scamp, of course I can hear!" Mr. Rogers trumpeted, going the colour of a

43

beetroot. Ned gave it up, but he was still puzzled; he could have sworn he had heard a cat mewing.

Ned and the cowman unloaded the boxes while Mr. Rogers's three children, who were on holiday from school, started filling them up with shining russet-and-crimson apples. Chequers heard people trampling all around him, crates being shoved and banged, and Gertie restlessly stamping her hoofs. He took a deep breath and howled at the top of his voice.

The cowman gave a startled yelp, dropped his crate on to his toe, and banged his head on one of the roof supports.

"'Elp, there's summat 'ere!" he gasped, hopping all over the cart on one leg.

Ned and the three children clustered round, and Ned wished he had the courage to say "I told you so!" to Mr. Rogers. Gertie stared round at them pityingly—fancy not recognizing Chequers's voice! Still, she was interested to see what would happen, and she pricked her ears and nickered encouragingly to him.

Gingerly the cowman lifted the crate that was shutting Chequers in, and something leaped upwards like a streak of greased lightning.

"Chequers!" yelled Ned, and made a wild grab

"Chequers!" yelled Ned, and made a wild grab as the streak shot from him, but Chequers wasn't going to be stopped by any meddling human, not after what he'd been through.

He landed on the ground and was off in a split

second, dodging between Gertie's legs as the children flung themselves after him. He didn't stop to look back, he just hurled himself on and on, past the haystack and under a gate, sending all the hens into hysterics, dashing through the middle of a calf-pen, in and out of the cart-shed and through the Dutch barn, with all the dogs in the place at his heels.

He saw another gate in front of him and he flung himself under it, whirled round to the right, tore along a hedgerow, and leaped through a gap in another hedge. The dogs went straight on, lost the scent, and after a little half-hearted questing, sauntered back to the farm looking very shamefaced and trying to pretend they hadn't been chasing anything at all.

Chequers, crouching low behind a nettle clump, angrily flicked his tail as he watched them. Then he heard Ned calling his name breathlessly, but he certainly wasn't going to take any notice. Besides, now he was here he wanted to explore.

He explored and explored, and it was wonderful.

46

He prowled down the edge of the ditch with a stealthiness that he felt fitted in with this strange place. At first he found it odd that there should be no houses, and, odder still, no people. Then he forgot to be surprised at anything, and just did as his forefathers all through the ages had done. He lifted each pad carefully and placed it so that no dry grass would rustle and no dead leaf crackle. He sniffed at hundreds of new scents, he heard new noises, and he saw new things.

He kept on and on, over a low wall at the end of the field, through a spinney, and then found himself by the banks of a fussy little stream that was just too broad to jump.

He couldn't get across so, of course, he wanted to, and he kept eyeing it and measuring the distance, but it grew broader instead of narrower in the most unhelpful fashion. It was only after he had gone quite a long way downstream (being a town cat he hadn't thought of going upstream) that he saw the willow-tree.

It was just made for climbing—Chequers could see

47

that at a glance, although he had never climbed one before—and what was more, one of the branches arched over the water in a perfect bridge. He took a running jump and fairly flew up the trunk. This was better even than roof-climbing! A flock of wood-pigeons went flapping away and a blackbird twittered wildly as Chequers tore madly up and down the branches, stopping dead on some bending bough with all his fur standing on end as if he had met a tiger face to face, then turning round like a tight-rope walker and slipping and sliding down to the ground again. He would fly for his life and hide behind a tree-trunk, peeping out to see if the coast was clear of imaginary enemies, and then, very cautiously, he would venture out again and go tearing up into the branches once more.

All at once he tired of it and sat down to lick himself thoughtfully. Then he remembered that he had wanted to cross the stream, and he sprang up on to the drooping branch. It was plain sailing till he was half-way across, but then the branch suddenly decided Chequers was too heavy for it. It swayed, dipped, and then gave up the fight and settled lower and lower. Chequers wobbled frantically, digging his claws into the bark, and watching the water come nearer and nearer. Now his front pads were getting wet, and the end of the branch was under water. He couldn't turn round and he couldn't go backwards—there was nothing for it but to jump. He jumped, but just as he thrust back with his hind legs the branch sagged unsteadily and Chequers landed with a splash a foot out from the bank. The water was horribly cold round his legs, and he paddled ashore, feeling furious.

Just before reaching the bank he decided that as he was in the water he might as well take a drink and that made him remember to feel hungry. He looked about vaguely, wondering what one did about food here, but as no one appeared with a saucer he decided he would have to do something about it himself.

He scrambled up the bank of the stream, glared at the treacherous willow-tree, and shook each leg separately and thoroughly. His hair clung to his legs, making them look ridiculously slim under his furry body. He started moving forward delicately, nose to ground, but although he picked up a dozen fascinating scents, not a fieldmouse or a vole did he see—he saw plenty of blackbirds and thrushes, though, and once a jay. They sat on twigs along the hedge, they flapped low over him, they watched him from the trees, and every one of them twittered or screamed their warning, for no matter how low he crouched or how carefully he screened himself behind nettle clumps or burr bushes, his black and white coat betrayed him.

At last he gave it up, but now he really was hungry, and it wasn't a nice feeling at all. He began to think about Mr. Sprigge and the two antique saucers with the black kittens round the edges (one for milk and the other for meat), and he remembered the nice easy-to-catch mice in the little shop—and how comfortable the cushion in the coal-scuttle was, too.

He was tired now, and he had a horrid suspicion

that it wasn't going to be simple finding his way back to Ned and Gertie and the cart. Still, he wouldn't think about that yet. At the moment all he wanted was to go to sleep. He saw a grass tuft with a hollow in the middle of it where a rabbit had lain to sun itself, and he pushed his way in, balled himself up nose to tail, closed his eyes, and was asleep.

While he slept the shadows were growing longer and longer and the sun sank lower until at last he hid himself behind a dark screen of clouds. The first owl woke up, stretching his wings sleepily and hooting as if he wanted to be sure his voice was still there.

It was the hoot that woke Chequers. He stirred drowsily, kneading his claws in and out as he used to do on the cushion back in Mr. Sprigge's shop, and blinked lazily. Then he sat up with a jerk and blinked again, thinking he must still be asleep. It was dark, but it wasn't the blackness of the shop and he wasn't in the old familiar coal-scuttle. He gazed up-wards, through the curving roof of grasses, to the grey night sky; he heard the wind sighing through the dry brown leaves and he heard the scuffling of the stream.

Now night had come it all seemed huge and unfriendly, different from the comfortable closeness of the moonlit roofs that he knew so well. A prickle ran along his skin, and he felt that he was very much alone.

Chapter V

GONE WILD

Chequers was wrong—he wasn't alone.

When he stayed quite still and listened, he heard a thousand tiny noises from every side, noises that told of scores of small creatures pattering to and fro, some feeding, some hunting, some carrying moss and fluff to make nests for their winter sleep, and some just enjoying them- selves.

The moment Chequers moved, his forgotten hunger woke up and seemed to burn a hole inside him. He licked his lips longingly and cautiously parted the screening grasses. Like a shadow he slipped towards the hedge, pausing to wrinkle his nose and sniff the scents the wind brought him. As he glided silently through the long grass, his black-and-white coat blended perfectly into the moonlight and the shadows—the piebald marking that was his enemy by day was his friend at night.

There was a sudden rustling in front of him and he froze into stillness, his eyes narrowed and glinting. A fieldmouse sat up to wash its whiskers, looking round warily at the same time, and then, satisfied, it started nibbling grass seeds.

There was a swish of dry grass as Chequers sprang, and then the beat of wings as an owl swooped low to investigate the sudden movement. Chequers raised his head and snarled throatily, and the startled owl sheered away with a shrill screech.

When he had eaten, Chequers moved noiselessly farther up the hedge, for one fieldmouse didn't make a supper. It wasn't till he had caught four that he was satisfied, and after lapping up a little of the cool, clear stream water he sought out a sleeping-place. He chose a gnarled old willow-tree whose knobbly top was splayed into a round seat just made for a cat's cubbyhole. He curled himself up, and before he slept he listened again to the stream and the gentle swishing of the willow leaves as they moved in the night breeze that ruffled his fur and left a cold, clean taste in his nostrils. He forgot that he had ever felt lonely or afraid; now he was happy.

For five days he lived by himself, lying up in the daytime in the willow-tree, or in the brown bracken that fringed the spinney, and hunting when darkness fell, or before the first flicker of sunlight broke through the blue-grey mistiness in the morning.

On the sixth day he woke as the stars were fading and heard a fox barking from somewhere across the stream. He shivered as the frosty wind nipped through his fur, and uncurled himself reluctantly. The trees in the spinney were russet now, and golden willow leaves drifted down to the surface of the water, where they whirled and twiddled and floated merrily down with the current.

Chequers watched them with his head on one side for an instant and then tore down the bank in a wild race, turning a somersault as he checked suddenly.

55

He stepped delicately out on to a flat stone and tried to catch the long, narrow leaves as they hurried past —it was fine fun until the stone shifted under him and

He tried to catch the long, narrow leaves as they hurried past

nearly tipped him head-first into the water. That made him decide it was too dangerous, and as he had caught one anyhow—it stuck persistently to his claw and he couldn't get rid of it—he pretended he had lost interest and stalked away towards the trees.

The carpet of dry leaves under his pads crackled

in the most inviting way, and he thought of the straw in the Dingles' barn, and Gertie. Just for old times' sake he romped madly, and then, panting and warm, he settled down to do something about breakfast.

He felt in the mood for adventure this morning, so he set off downstream with his tail held low, his ears half back to catch the slightest sound and a purposeful expression on his face.

After about a hundred yards the spinney ended abruptly, but the stream scurried on and down a dip in a stony hill-side dotted with bramble bushes and stunted hawthorns. As Chequers slipped through the paling at the edge of the trees and started down the hill-side there was a sudden chorus of shrill bleating, a scamper of hoofs, and dark shapes that he had taken for bushes rose up and stampeded away from him.

He didn't know it was a flock of sheep he had disturbed, but whatever they were, they had scared his breakfast away with their silly stamping and bleating.

He snarled after them in the most throaty and grown-up manner—when hunting he was anything but a kitten—and broke into an easy lope. It was no good trying any serious stalking in this neighbourhood, and as the sheep had wheeled downhill, following the stream, he struck out across the slope to keep as far away from them as possible.

He was ravenous by now, and he knew there wasn't much time before the sun would be up. Even now there were palest lemon streaks in the heavy blue masses of cloud in the east, and soon the blackbirds and thrushes would be awake and warning the world that the piebald hunter was on the warpath.

In a flash he was crouching tensely in the grass beside a briar rose-bush, his eyes glued on a gap between two bramble clumps.

He knew something had moved there a moment before, but as he waited and waited and still nothing happened, he grew doubtful. At that moment the first thin rays of the sun came slanting between the hills, gleaming on the wet grass, strengthening every minute until the trees and the bushes were picked out in a warm yellow glow. The first birds sleepily tried out their voices, and Chequers sank lower into the friendly grass, feeling hungrier and hungrier.

Suddenly he stiffened, his eyes snapped open, and he bunched his hind legs under him. A rabbit, its jaws working busily, had lolloped out from the very gap in the brambles that he had been watching.

Chequers lost no time. He drew back and hurled himself outwards in a perfect spring that landed him just where the rabbit had been—but it wasn't there now.

Something was there, though, something with teeth like needles that sank into Chequers's fore leg. The stoat was just about as surprised as Chequers at first, for he had been aiming at the rabbit too. He had leaped just a second before, but the rabbit had seen him and bolted at the last moment. Then this large black-and-white thing had arrived, also, apparently, with the same idea, and the stoat, who was bloodthirsty by nature, took it as a signal to start a battle.

Chequers took longer to sort out his ideas, but when he did start he made up for lost time. He squirmed over on to his back and tore savagely with

The stoat darted in again, but Chequers was ready this time

his hind claws at the stoat's underside. The stoat let go his hold, sprang away, and then darted in again, but Chequers was ready this time and he jerked sideways. As the stoat flashed by him he lashed out with

60

his fore paws. There was a stabbing pain in his ear, but Chequers was past caring. Instinctively he snapped his teeth home on the back of the stoat's neck and hung on as his enemy twisted and threshed. Suddenly the stoat used his emergency weapon. A smell worse than Chequers could ever have imagined hit him like a wave and his first thought was to fly as fast as his legs would carry him.

Then, as the stoat twisted and snapped again, he hung on grimly. Suddenly his enemy went limp in his jaws, and Chequers glared round, trying to see where the smell was coming from. It was everywhere, and he couldn't make it out at all, so, still clutching the dead stoat, he leaped away between the bramble bushes. The smell followed him, seeming to grow worse instead of better, and all at once he realized. He dropped the stoat like a red-hot poker and fled.

He didn't stop till he had reached the other side of the field and he couldn't go any farther because of the pain in the fore leg the stoat had bitten. The

61

moment he stood still he found the smell was still with him, and then, to his horror, he realized it was on *him*. If Chequers had been a little more experienced he would have known that even foxes and badgers never attack a stoat, for they know his weapon, and they know the smell lingers for days.

Chequers was miserable. He found an old mole-hill and rolled in the dry powdery earth, he rubbed his face in the grass, he pushed himself down into heaps of dead leaves under the hedge, but nothing did the slightest bit of good. He was hungry, too, and his leg was so painful that he could hardly put it down.

There was no chance now of breakfast, and he knew it only too well, although he did half-heartedly try stalking, but his injured leg made it difficult to move quietly and the awful smell gave him away almost as badly as his colouring. At last he gave it up in despair and sat down to lick his wounds. Then he tried to sleep, but that was no good either, and he limped unhappily down by the side of the hedgerow, sniffing hungrily at all the inviting scents.

By midday he was in a bad state, hobbling on three legs, spattered with blood from his torn ear and his leg, his once beautiful fur matted and tangled with burrs and grasses and dead leaves from his desperate rolling.

Suddenly he flattened himself to the ground, his eyes wide with fear, for he had heard a man's voice. Somehow after his six days on his own he had come to fear man, and now, of all times, he wanted to be left alone.

The voice came nearer, and then Chequers crouched back hissing as through a gap in the hedge just in front of him a man appeared, dressed in an ancient blue shirt, moleskin waiscoat, and corduroys.

"Hey, what might you be a-doin' here?" the shepherd called, his quick eyes taking in the matted fur and the flecks of blood. Then he raised his voice, still watching Chequers. "Master Joe, nip through

63

the gap farther up, lad, I've got a cat yere as looks in a bad way."

Chequers heard someone running along the far side of the hedge, and he felt trapped.

He turned and hobbled as fast as he could for the shelter of a bramble patch, but he wasn't quick enough. A boy burst through another gap and headed him downhill, and he couldn't move fast enough to dodge the shepherd. A huge brown hand shot out and gripped him by the scruff of the neck, swinging him up into the air as if he was a tiny kitten again in Mr. Dingle's loft. He drew his lips back defiantly, but as the big, strangely gentle hands shifted their hold, he felt he didn't want to bite or scratch. He lay still, nestling against the soft moleskin, and let the shepherd look at his injured paw and his ear.

The boy, Joe, wanted to stroke him, but the shepherd wrinkled his nose and grinned, shaking his head.

"No, Master Joe, don't you come too near. You can whiff him a mile away, eh? And I don't know

64

what your ma would say if you came 'ome reekin' like a midden. Fightin' with a stoat most likely, and he ain't much more'n a kitten by the looks of 'im."

The shepherd ruffled the long black-and-white fur, and Chequers closed his eyes and ventured an experimental purr as a large finger started tickling him under the chin. His purring grew stronger and he began to feel very safe and contented.

"What d'you think happened—how did he get here?" Joe shot out the questions eagerly, dancing round in excitement.

"Well, reckon he quarrelled with Master Stoat over summat to eat, and as to how he come to be a-huntin' yere, why, there's no tellin' as to what cats will do. But look'ee, Master Joe, see these yere burrs? If he'd been wild fer long, they'd be buried deep in his fur, worked right down close to his skin, and all that white fur'd be a sight dirtier than it is now. There'd be knots all over 'im—long-'aired cats gets themselves in a terrible mess a'fore you can say Jack Robinson. When I were no bigger'n you I saw a

Persian cat as had run off by 'erself, and mostly all 'er fur had to come off.''

"Oh, Bob," wailed Joe, "you won't have to do it this time, will you?"

"Bless you no, Master Joe. That's what I said— these be surface tangles, showin' he ain't been out long, and they'll come out easy when we gets to work on 'em wi' a comb!"

"What are you going to do with him, Bob?" said Joe rather breathlessly, secretly aching to have Chequers for his own.

"Put summat on this leg of his for a start," chuckled the shepherd, watching Joe with his eyes twinkling. "And then, when he don't smell no more, how'd you like to have 'im, Master Joe?"

"Can I, Bob, really? Gosh, do take the smell off quickly!" Joe implored, in the seventh heaven of delight.

Bob laughed and promised he'd do his best, and then sent Joe tearing downhill to the cottage to get Mrs. Bob to have some hot water and strips of old linen ready.

Bob didn't approve of cats that went wild, for he knew that in the spring they might be a danger to the lambs, but he could see Chequers was only a kitten and probably new to the game—and anyway, Bob was the sort of person who helped things that needed helping.

CHAPTER VI

THE RIVER

Chequers was almost asleep when they reached the cottage, but he woke up with a bump when he smelled the dinner Mrs. Bob was cooking.

She must have been a thought-reader, for the moment she saw him she exclaimed, "Ah, the poor thing, I'm sure he's simply starving!" and bustled off to find all the things that cats dream about, and never said a word about the smell.

Chequers lapped and munched and purred in uncertain, hiccupy gulps while Bob put a little disinfectant into the water. It was painful while the bites were being cleaned, but Chequers was very good, and by the time he had filled himself out to bursting point and was bandaged up tidily, he was blissful.

Mrs. Bob produced a comb and was just about to brave the smell and start smartening Chequers up, but Bob said it was better one of them should reek, not two. When Bob had finished, Chequers was his old, beautiful self once more, and he lay in the sun and slept till the evening, when he wolfed a large and tasty supper.

It was four days before the smell wore off, and his leg had almost healed too. His ear was quite all right, except that it would always have a jagged edge, and that was what made Joe call him "Tag".

On the fifth day Joe came up to the cottage with a basket with a cushion in it, and triumphantly started carrying Chequers down to the farm as if he was a piece of fragile porcelain. Chequers was feeling so well that half-way there he objected and plunged out of the basket. His leg gave him a nasty twinge as he landed on the ground, but after that he felt fine and went scudding uphill back to Bob's cottage.

There was a fine game of hide-and-seek (he was in a kittenish mood), and at last Joe had to scale an apple-tree and grab him as he teetered on the topmost bough.

After a little more trouble Joe tied a ball of news-paper on a string and set off trailing it behind him like a tail and whistling jauntily as if he had forgotten all about Chequers. That did the trick. Chequers was outraged at being overlooked and hared along after the paper, catching it and rolling over and over with it held tightly against his tummy—and without know-ing it, he was lured right down to the farm.

When he was there he suddenly realized he had been tricked, but Joe was taking no chances and scooped him up into his arms. After he had been introduced to Mr. and Mrs. Cranley, Chequers was taken up to Joe's room and shown his bed—a cushion in an old dog-basket—and his saucers. Joe left him to nose around and pelted downstairs to beg a bit of butter from his mother, but when he arrived upstairs again, Chequers was gone.

Joe was bitterly disappointed, and leaving the butter on the window-sill, started hunting wildly. The butter began to melt in the sun, and Chequers, who had merely been exploring along the guttering,

Joe set off, trailing the string behind him

came back, ate it, and settled down for a nap in his basket, where Joe, hot and dishevelled, found him an

Chequers came back and ate the butter

hour later, after having almost given up the search in despair. Joe was sad at not being able to smear the butter on Chequers's pads, but his mother said it probably worked as well inside as out.

Chequers settled down almost at once—that is, he dropped in for meals and turned up at odd moments for a nap in the basket. In a few days he had trained them all not to take any notice of his sudden disappearances, and he found an exciting way down to the ground from Joe's window, which made it easy to dodge in and out unexpectedly.

Sometimes he went up the hill-side to visit Bob and his wife, and often he hunted—sometimes mice and rats in the barns and the rick-yard, sometimes water rats by the pond and along the stream, and sometimes field-mice and voles along the hedgerows or among the thick grass tussocks. As autumn turned into winter he learned lots of things, and he was growing up fast. He was big now, and his long fur (kept silkily smooth with a little assistance from Joe) made him look larger still. He had filled out, too, and his ears and his pads were the right size for the rest of him instead of being too large.

When winter came he stayed by the farm more, for the hunting was poor now that the field-mice had balled themselves up in their holes to sleep. The mice round the barns still scurried and nibbled, but the only trouble was that Chequers had to share them with two other cats—a huge black tom who thought himself cock of the roost, and a small scared-looking grey cat who hunted like a gliding shadow and never missed a kill, fading discreetly into the background whenever the tom was anywhere about.

Chequers got on rather well with the grey shadow, but from the moment he met the black bully they were sworn enemies. After a skirmish over a particularly plump rat that Chequers had killed, in which he gave as good as he got, and sent the black creature loping away with a scratched nose, they reached a sort of working agreement. If the black bully happened to be lying in ambush among the straw bales, Chequers would take one look and vanish in the direction of the cartshed. Grey Shadow never got in anybody's way.

Chequers didn't like the winter; he prefered roaming farther afield than the yard and the garden, and one day when the weather seemed milder he set out defiantly to visit Bob and do a little real hunting—as it was his first winter he had no idea how long it would last, and every time he thought it was warmer he kept hoping that animals to hunt would have woken up.

He was out of luck, and as he came out on to the open hill-side a bitter wind cut into him, tugging at his bushy tail and nipping through his fur like a knife. He dodged back through the hedge and decided to lie up in a hollow tree for his midday sleep, and then go home.

Two hours later he woke, and after he had blinked his eyes open he gazed about him in horror.

Something terrible had happened to the world—it was white!

The snow was still falling and he watched it silently, trying to puzzle it out. Then suddenly he realized that the snowflakes looked like little balls of white paper, just made to play with.

He somehow didn't think they were paper, though,

otherwise they would have rustled when they dropped, and these were so silent that it was almost dreamlike. Even the whining wind had dropped and the white-powdered trees and bushes stood still as if they were frozen, with never a twig moving.

Chequers decided that if he didn't move soon he would be frozen too. He crouched back, marking an extra fat snowflake as it came drifting down, and then sprang at it. He was sure he hadn't missed it, but when he opened his claws and peered down it was nowhere to be seen. Then he realized that the white stuff underneath him was cold and damp, and he lifted each leg in turn and shook them daintily, but as he had to put them back on the snow again it didn't do much good.

He put his head down and smelled the stuff, but jerked away as his nose touched it. He tried to investigate the flakes that settled on his coat, showing up so clearly on his black patches and hiding themselves where he was white, but it was no good. They just disappeared the moment he touched them, and when

76

he tried to eat some they nearly froze up his tongue. He felt they weren't quite playing the game.

There was nothing for it but to go home, and it

The flakes just disappeared the moment he touched them

wasn't a pleasant journey. He kept blundering into hollows where he sank up to his tummy, and even where it was only an inch or so deep it wetted his legs, clotting the hairs together and matting the long feathering on his beautiful tail.

The snow lay for a few days, and Joe was secretly

pleased, because he had Chequers more to himself than before, but for his part, Chequers simply sulked.

It seemed ages before the days really began to grow warmer, and then, of course, it rained. Chequers was in a fever of impatience; he felt in his bones that spring had come and he ought to be out and catching things before everybody else—that meant the black bully—had caught them, and he sat on the window-sill glaring at the dismal view, or padding up and down like a piebald panther in a cage.

Then it cleared; damp-looking strips of blue sky were uncovered as the sodden clouds fled before the wind and the weak sun flickered out. Chequers saw it out of the corner of his eye and leaped out of Joe's arms, pelted across the sitting-room floor, and squeezed through the door just as Mrs. Cranley was opening it to call Joe for lunch.

The window in the hall was open, and he leaped through it, banging his legs on the sill. Now he was out—and the air smelled sweet and damp and clean. He wrinkled his nose and sifted the scents that came to him, tantalizing scents that made him want to split himself up into a dozen bits so that he could follow all of them. The wind was coming from the west, and he decided he would head into it—that showed he was more experienced, for he knew he could scent his quarry without being winded himself.

He crossed the yard, crept under the gate, and started loping along the hedge. The grass was wet, but he was enjoying himself far too much to bother about that, and he padded steadily on, not worrying about taking cover. He didn't care how loud the birds twittered their warnings now; he wanted to get well away from the farm before he settled down to business.

Half-way down the second field, when a couple of thrushes and a plover were screaming their heads off just above him, he dived into the middle of the hedge and lay low till the commotion had finished. When everything was quiet he prowled noiselessly along a rabbit track that ran, tunnel-like, between the gnarled branches. Before he had gone a hundred yards he caught a shrew, but as it had a peculiar musky scent he left it and moved on, angrily twitching his tail. Next he surprised two field-mice, one after the other, and it was so simple that he began to get bored.

When he had reached the end of the field, which was the farthest he had been before, he stopped and considered. There was a little imp of mischief inside him to-day, and he made up his mind to explore. This was different country to the steep, stony hill-sides where Bob's sheep munched and bleated; it was flatter here, with elm-trees dotting the hedgerows, and fields of kale, mangolds, and new wheat on either side.

Chequers wriggled through the next hedge and skipped across a lane. A stream cut across the field on the far side, and he loped towards it, hoping for water rats, but it was too open and in broad daylight he didn't stand a chance. Still, he wasn't particularly hungry, and it was fun just exploring, so he kept on. There was a low line of willows ahead and to the left a huddle of sheds, two cranes, and stacks and stacks

80

of timber. A lorry came bumping along a cinder-track on the other side of the stream, sending out showers of muddy yellow water on each side of its wheels as it sloshed through the puddles, and Chequers watched it pull up by one of the sheds. He wasn't interested in the timber yard, but he was interested in the willows—once screened by them it wouldn't matter if he was red, white, and blue.

He broke into a canter, but when he was a couple of yards away from the trees he paused, eyeing them uncertainly. Dirty-looking brown water was lapping all round them so that they formed a long narrow island of dark twigs feathered with pale young leaves. Chequers had never seen a river before and he didn't realize that it wasn't usually like this, but the rains had swelled it until it had risen almost to the top of the shallow grassy bank where he stood. He eyed it thoughtfully, not quite liking the sullen way it swirled past him, but he set off along the bank to try to find some willows that weren't under water.

He came to an opening in the trees and stared

across at a barge being loaded with timber by one of the cranes. He moved a little farther, across a wooden jetty where a couple more lorries were parked, skirted the concrete and steel base of the crane, and squeezed through a gap in some chestnut paling.

The bank was higher now, and underneath it two barges lay moored, waiting their turn to be filled. Their cave-like holds looked dark and exciting, and Chequers wavered from one leg to the other, wishing he could jump across.

He didn't know that the loose soil of the bank had been eaten away by the swirling flood water and he didn't notice more and more earth plop-plopping into the river. He balanced himself on the very edge, wondering if he dared to risk the jump—and then, before he knew what was happening, the grass under him had given way and in the next second he was in the water.

CHAPTER VII

TUG-BOAT CAT

He sank for an instant, and then his head bobbed up again. Instinctively he struck out with his fore legs, beating the water frantically, straining to get back to the bank, but the current was too strong and he was swept away, under the overhanging black stern of the barge, farther and farther out towards midstream.

He still threshed wildly and managed to keep his head above water, but he was more afraid than he had ever been in his life. He was so low he could see nothing but the hurrying brown ripples, but all at once his wildly staring eyes caught sight of something dark and solid creeping up on his right. He thrust desperately with all his legs and heaved himself forward. The plank was level with him now, but the current was carrying it swiftly and in a moment it would be past. He gave another heave, and a freak of the current swept him closer. He clawed at it and hung on, trailing beside it, and then, inch by inch, he dragged himself on to it.

He lay there gasping, coughing, and sneezing

He was too wet and weary and miserable to do anything but lie there gasping, coughing, and sneezing to get rid of the water he had swallowed, and he didn't see the squat red-funnelled tug alter her course and swing towards him.

84

The skipper had seen something black and white in the water, and as he had no clumsy string of barges trailing behind him, he had decided to take a look. When the thing started crawling up on to the drifting plank the skipper knew it was something out of the ordinary, and he yelled for Alf to stand by with the boat-hook.

George, who combined being cook with all the odd jobs anyone could think of, came up on deck to throw a bucket of dishwater overboard, and paused when he saw the *Ladybird* heading in towards the bank. He saw Alf brandishing the boat-hook and then he caught sight of the plank and the bedraggled pie-bald object crouching on it.

"Easy with that boat-'ook, Alf, me boy!" he said, grabbing it before Alf could protest. "'Ere, lemme do it. Nah, you lean over an' ketch a hold o' the h'object, while I brings the timber alongside. I'll be 'anging on to yer coat-tails!"

Chequers raised his head as the squat black shape of the tug slid gradually nearer. He saw men leaning over the side, and he opened his mouth and mewed for the first time.

"All right, me 'earty! Won't be long nah!" shouted George cheerfully, and measuring the distance with a careful eye, he made a dive with the boat-hook and guided the plank skilfully into the side.

Alf dangled precariously head downward, and Chequers saw a pair of large grimy hands stretching towards him. Then he was seized, and George hauled both of them back on board.

While Chequers lay quite still, dripping water down Alf's waistcoat, George summed the situation up in a glance, dropped the boat-hook, grabbed Chequers, and darted towards the cubby-hole that he called his galley.

Things happened to Chequers so fast that he gave up trying to keep pace with them and just let George bully him. He was balled up in a towel and rubbed till he tingled, and then something hot and fiery was poured into his mouth, which made him feel most peculiar but rather nice, and warmed him up as if he had a stove inside him.

George fussed over him like an anxious hen, and

Chequers was well and truly tucked in

wasn't satisfied till he had made a nest at one end of his bunk and seen that Chequers was well and truly tucked in. Then he went on deck and reported to the skipper.

"I reckon 'e's nice lookin', too, when 'e's dry," George wound up, watching the skipper out of the corner of his eye.

"Humph," said the skipper. "Wonder where he comes from?"

"Shouldn't think we'll ever know," said George hopefully.

"Humph," retorted the skipper again, knowing perfectly well what George wanted. "More fool him to fall in!"

George invented half a dozen reasons why any self-respecting cat could fall in, and the skipper gave in at last.

"Well," he chuckled, "it's your business to see he doesn't get in the way, and now he's one o' the crew, no more 'catfish' stunts, see!"

George departed, grinning happily at having settled things so nicely, but there was just one thing he had forgotten: he hadn't consulted Chequers.

Chapter VIII

THE CIRCUS

They chugg-chugged comfortably down-river, carried on by the current, and tied up in the evening at the docks. Chequers didn't stir till then, and when he did he felt so dazed that he could hardly remember what had happened to him.

He hadn't lost his appetite though, and he woke up soon enough when he smelled the enormous meal George had prepared for him. After he had eaten and lain purring on George's lap to be combed, he began to feel more himself and resisted all efforts to get him to go to sleep in the bunk again. George took it as a good sign and proudly watched while Chequers padded across the deck, investigated the wheel-house, and worked his way aft till he stood peering over the stern into the dark, greenish water that slipped past them towards the sea.

7

89

George was having visions of fishing Chequers out again and opened his mouth to call him back, but he needn't have worried. One swim was enough, and Chequers wasn't taking any chances.

He curled up in George's bunk that night, and in the morning before daylight he had a look at the silent, oil-smeared engines down below. They didn't smell like the sort of place for rats or mice, so he wasn't interested in them, but the deck-house seemed more hopeful. Before he had time to get bored, mouth-watering smells of kippers began wafting into every corner of the *Ladybird*, and Chequers scampered back to the galley to share in the vast breakfast George had prepared for himself and Tom, who looked after the engines. Just as they had finished, the skipper and Alf, who lived near the docks, came clattering on board, and when Tom had raised steam they nosed out into mid-river and then chugged down a little farther to wait for some barges to finish loading. Chequers didn't understand all the moving up and down and shifting of barges here and there, but at last they were really off.

It was slow work thud-thudding their way upstream with a heavy load, and it wasn't till evening that they reached the wharf where the barges would be unloaded. Chequers cast a loving eye towards the shore, for he was finding the tug just a little small, and as soon as George's back was turned he leaped from the *Ladybird*'s stern up the wooden steps leading up to the jetty.

Up there he was happy. He stalked rats round the grain elevators, he climbed about underneath an old jetty, and he pattered along the canvas-covered hatches of a string of barges moored head to tail beside a row of warehouses. He saw other cats, mostly lean and furtive, but when he left the wharves and prowled over the house-roofs he saw a different sort—fat, well-cared-for cats like the ones he had so admired when he was still a kitten at Mr. Sprigge's antique shop. He listened to them serenading—he hadn't heard a cat concert since his wanderings had started—and he suddenly felt he would like to sing too.

He selected a likely looking party and started gently, for he wasn't quite sure of his voice. The largest cat seemed to object to a new-comer interrupting but Chequers dealt with him most satisfactorily. He began to think himself a very fine fellow, but it was strange how humans never seemed to appreciate the same sort of singing as cats did, and when someone bellowed at them from an open window and shone a torch on to them he fled only just in time before a cascade of water spattered over the gable.

He wandered farther, but he was beginning to feel tired now. On either side of him stretched a maze of roofs, and it was pitch dark, for the moon was hidden by clouds. Chequers stood quite still and thought hard. He had been along so many walls and gutterings, and up and down so many gables that he began to realize that he wasn't quite sure of the way back. He sniffed the breeze, but it didn't help him, and he

He leapt from the *Ladybird*'s stern up the wooden steps

started up the ridge in front of him to see if he could get his bearings from the top.

At the crest he paused, sniffing eagerly. It wasn't the river he smelled—it was something much more exciting to him—something that made him think of the old days when he was a kitten. For a moment he couldn't make it out, and then he remembered—Gertie!

The horse smell rose up to him, strong and fragrant, and he slithered down the steep roof to try to get nearer to it, forgetting all about the tug. He had to make a half-circle before he could find a wall low enough to drop down, and then he followed his nose —along an alleyway, through a gap in a hoarding, across a deserted car park, under a gate—and found himself in a stretch of open ground.

He stared round, puzzled, looking for a narrow yard with a barn and a stable like Gertie's, but there was nothing like that here, and yet the horse smell was everywhere. There was a line of big lorries and vans parked ahead of him, and he trotted towards

94

them with his head on one side, one ear back, and the other forward. Then he saw a low tent, and from it came the old familiar sounds that he knew so well— the rattle of a head-chain, the stamp of an impatient hoof—best of all, the rustle of straw.

He broke into a canter and skidded round the corner of the tent trying to find an opening. The canvas hung loosely across the entrance and he pushed swiftly past it and stood gazing round him.

This was a different stable from the one he knew, with its wooden stall, the ladder up to the loft, its brick floor and the piles of crates. Here a line of poles ran down the middle, striped and banded with colours—he could see that in the dim light of a hurricane lamp standing on a stool beside the dark huddle of a sleeping man. On either side of the tent were horses, fetlock deep in yellow crackling straw, and above them, hanging on each side of the poles, was harness that would have given Gertie a fit if she had seen it—broad red-and-yellow girths, bridles and headstalls studded with silver and brass, and bright fuzzy plumes.

Chequers padded softly past a pair of Shetland ponies, a zebra, a mule, four roan liberty horses, and two old nags, so fat that they looked as if they could never heave themselves into a rocking-horse canter. All of them were asleep—the zebra, the mule, and one of the Shetlands lying down, and the others standing like statues, with drooping heads and closed eyes—but suddenly Chequers knew he was being watched.

He swung towards the farthest end of the tent and saw a head stretched over a canvas partition and a wild, angry eye rolling back at him so that the white showed.

There were no plumes hung up here and no fantastic headstalls or girths, but a plain saddle, polished till it gleamed, and a simple bridle hung over a wooden bar, and above the stall the name "Zulu" was painted in gold letters on a black varnished board.

96

Chequers moved forward, his curiosity getting the better of him, and the horse snorted, twitching his ears back, but Chequers wasn't daunted. None of the other horses looked in the least like Gertie, and this giant didn't really, except for one thing—he was black too, with a white blaze on his forehead, a delicately pink nose, and four white stockings (Gertie only had two, but Chequers didn't worry about that).

He gave a little "Prrrr?" of introduction, and the great horse glared at him, twisted his neck round with a rattle of his head-chain, and blew threateningly. The whole thing was so completely like the first time he had met Gertie that Chequers began to feel utterly happy and quite at home—he knew suddenly that he would never go back to the tug.

He wasn't even bothered when the great beast sidled away from him, snorting and stamping; in fact, he thought it was very considerate as it gave him more room to take a header into the straw.

He bunched himself back against the canvas partition and catapulted towards the rustling golden

97

carpet, turning a double somersault from sheer high
spirits. He had forgotten all about being tired and

Zulu threw his head up, his eyes rolling and his ears flat

he played until he could play no more, doing all the
old kittenish things, clutching wisps in his fore paws
and tearing them with his hind feet, hunting feverishly
for invisible mice, and pretending to be terrified out

98

of his wits by the moving shadows cast by the lantern on the tent walls when they billowed inwards with the wind.

Nearer and nearer he rolled to the far side of the stall where Zulu stood, wide-eyed and snorting, twitching his ears back and then pricking them forward. Chequers looked up casually as he bumped against one hind hoof, and Zulu shuddered as if he had been stung.

For a moment he hunched his back and threw his head up, his eyes rolling and his ears flat. If he had wanted to he knew he could have torn the whole flimsy tent down and stamped this strange creature flat—but did he want to? He didn't know.

For once in his life he was flummoxed, so he stood for a second to see what happened, still trembling and sweating behind his ears. Chequers gave another "Prrrr?" wondering why his new friend looked so worried, and then settled down to wash himself.

That finished Zulu. He simply stood and goggled. He put his head down and breathed great gales of hay-scented breath over Chequers, who suddenly decided to turn round and tickled Zulu's nose with his waving tail. The great black head jerked away

His nose was nowhere near the water

and a hoof stamped threateningly, but even that didn't move Chequers, who had now decided he was thirsty and strolled across to the blue-and-yellow bucket standing in the corner. It was almost empty, and his nose was nowhere near the water even when he stood on tiptoe. He gave a heave and swung for a

100

moment, balancing with his tummy on the rim of the bucket. Of course it upset—at his age he ought to have known better—and he was only able to lick up a few drops before it all sank through the straw into the earth.

The clatter woke the sleeping groom, but he was so used to disturbances coming from Zulu's end of the tent that he only rolled over, muttering, and went to sleep again. By now Zulu was fascinated; he had completely forgotten about tearing things down, and he didn't even flinch when Chequers brushed against him and flopped down half on top of his hoof. Chequers wasn't still for long, though—the hoof wasn't a soft enough pillow—and he eventually sprawled out at the bottom of Zulu's feed-box.

He opened one eye reluctantly as the great black head was lowered, and he flicked his tail as the velvety pink muzzle nudged him gently. Then he slept.

CHAPTER IX

CHEQUERS GETS A JOB

It was Finnegan, Zulu's little Irish groom, who found him next morning. Finnegan's eyes nearly popped out of his head and for once in his life he couldn't think of anything to say. He backed out of Zulu's stall, puffing and blowing as if someone had thrown a bucket of cold water over him, and he grabbed Smithie, the groom who slept in the tent, by the arm.

"Smithie!" he gasped. "Would ye look at that an' tell me if it's dreamin' I am!"

Smithie looked cautiously over the partition and gave a long whistle. Zulu flung his head up and his ears flashed back.

"Shteady, bhoy, shteady," soothed Finnegan, and Chequers, hearing his voice, woke up, yawned, and proceeded to stretch himself lazily before he hopped out of the feed-box and looked inquiringly up over the partition.

Finnegan opened his mouth, shut it again, and swallowed. Five years he'd been looking after Zulu, and he'd seen him wreck the tent twice, break loose six times, and generally get such a reputation that no one except Finnegan, who loved him like his own child, and Mr. Russell, who owned him, would go near him.

Now here was this harlequin of a piebald creature walking, cool as you please, between Zulu's fore legs —faith and bejabers, if Smithie hadn't seen it too it was mad he'd think he was!

Chequers decided it was time to find out about breakfast, and headed for the end of the stall. Zulu craned round and nickered anxiously, and Chequers looked back, quirking his tail as if to say "Cheerio, shan't be long".

"Faith!" breathed Finnegan, and then as Chequers trotted down the tent towards the entrance he jumped into action. Things like this didn't happen twice— if Zulu wanted a cat for a friend, a cat he should have, and Finnegan wasn't going to see this piebald magician disappear just when he had started working his magic.

He tried to remember what cats ate—he had never had much to do with them and he could only think in terms of oats, and hay, and bran mashes. Then he heard a throaty roar as one of the lions across in the cage-wagon woke up, and that gave him an inspiration. Over by the wagon, Don Lopez, the trainer (Bill Billings in private life), was busy getting the lions' breakfast ready, and snatching up a tin plate Finnegan raced towards him.

Meanwhile Chequers strolled slowly across the dry withered grass, yawning again, stretching himself, and digging his claws into the earth. Cooking smells came from all round him—it was Sunday, and the circus wouldn't be moving to the next pitch till later in the day, so for once they could breakfast in peace.

The whole space was dotted with vans and lorries and converted motor buses, most of them gaily painted with blue and yellow. Chequers bristled as another gurgling, hungry roar came from the long, barred cage-wagon, and then he stood, turning round slowly, wondering which cooking smell seemed the most promising.

Everything looked most exciting—he had never seen houses on wheels before, or such an odd assortment of strange animals. There was a pair of vast grey elephants, a woolly black and white llama, two goats, a troupe of monkeys in a big wire cage mounted on a van, and he could hear the voices of a dozen different dogs.

While he was making up his mind which way to go he allowed himself to be stroked by one or two of the men who were hurrying backwards and forwards from the lorries, packing away poles, and seating, and odd-shaped bundles of canvas. He had just decided to head for a large green and white trailer when he heard someone running behind him. He swung round and saw it was Finnegan—but what interested him most was the chunk of lion's breakfast Finnegan was carrying.

Chequers purred and waved his tail gracefully—
how thoughtful people were!—and let himself be led
back to the horse-tent where he munched happily
while Zulu was fed too.

He was still eating when he heard Finnegan be-
seeching someone to "belave me, for indade 'tis cold
sober that I am". It was Dan Russell, who owned
Zulu and rode him in an "haute école" act—Zulu
was one of the circus stars, and he knew all about
bowing to the audience, pirouetting on his hind legs,
and waltzing in time to music.

"Will ye come an' see for yerself, sorr," said
Finnegan in the end, and Dan came, and saw, and
wondered.

"But supposing he belongs to someone about here,"
Dan said doubtfully. "He's a beauty, aren't you,
boy?" Chequers looked up in agreement; he knew
from Dan's voice that he was being talked about, and
he loved admiration. He decided Dan was the right
sort of person and pushed himself against his legs.

Finnegan chuckled.

"Made himself at home, hasn't he? Don't you worry, sorr, lave it to me entirely! Shure, anyone's free to join a circus—and he came of his own free will, didn't he, now?"

Chequers lay in the straw to wash himself

At that moment Zulu looked round with ears cocked and nickered gently. Chequers licked up the last scrap of the milk that Finnegan had produced from somewhere, and then went and lay in the straw to wash himself.

That settled it. Chequers joined the circus.

Chapter X

"HARLEQUIN" AND "COLUMBINE"

After breakfast they started pulling down the horse-tent, and Smithie and Bill Billings's son, Ted, set off for the next pitch, each riding one horse and leading two others. The Shetlands, the zebra, and the mule, together with the goats and the llama, were to ride in state in a van. The elephants had started earlier, as they were so slow. Finnegan saddled up Zulu, and Dan mounted him, but Zulu was in a rage because he thought Chequers was being left behind, and there was quite a little tussle before he started. Finnegan swooped on Chequers, who showed signs of wanting to go off and explore, and to his fury he was shut up in Dan's living-wagon.

He loathed it when they started off—it reminded him too much of that awful ride inside the box in Gertie's cart. When at last they stopped he waited behind the door till Dan came to open it, and then shot out like an arrow before he could be stopped, and nothing would make him wait to be caught.

He found they had pulled up in the middle of a field and he made a note of the most likely hunting-grounds for the evening, but at the moment he wanted to investigate all the wagons and lorries, and find out what the tent-men were doing.

He managed to get in everyone's way and was nearly smothered when the wind pulled a strip of canvas down on top of him. He watched, awestruck, as the towering king pole of the big tent was hauled into position, and he fled for his life when one of the lions opened its huge red mouth and roared at him. He hadn't investigated a quarter of all the exciting things when he started feeling hungry, and trotted towards the horse-tent. Zulu let out a ringing whinny of welcome, which set everything else in the tent dancing madly (except the nags, who were too fat and lazy). Finnegan had wangled some more meat from Bill Billings and had milked one of the goats

when no one was looking. Chequers purred contentedly and settled down. Goat's milk was a little
strange at first but he was too ravenous to bother.

While Dan practised Zulu in the ring Chequers
went round making friends with everybody from the
tent-men to the owner. Everyone had a little something left over from lunch, and by the time he had
finished he was blown out like a barrel.

Hordes of children were swarming round the circus
field, and as they all wanted to play with Chequers,
the only thing to do was to take refuge in Zulu's stall;
anyway, after his large meal he was only too pleased
to sprawl lazily in the straw. Then as soon as it was
dark he went out on a long, serious and very success-
ful hunt, and it was midnight before he slipped back
into the horse-tent again.

There were more people on the Monday, especially
in the afternoon, when they flocked to see the menagerie before the first show at four. Then the band
started thumping and blaring inside the big top,
and tent-men (suddenly very grand in blue-and-gold

uniforms) bustled to and fro shepherding the queue and seeing that the "shillings" didn't squeeze in among the "half-crowns".

At first Chequers couldn't understand the clowns at all—people he had made friends with yesterday and whose scent he knew, suddenly appeared with different faces—and what faces!—and expected him to remember them. He sniffed them carefully before he decided they were the same people; there were a lot of things that were strange here, but he supposed that as all humans were mad anyway, these must be just a little more so than usual—but they were quite nice and very thoughtful about food.

When they moved early the next morning Chequers saw to it that he rode on the lorry that carried the horse-tent—no more stuffy trailers for him. He sat on top of the stacks of poles and canvas and planks, and as he let the wind ruffle through his fur he felt content.

He began to work out his days into a routine—travelling on the lorry, making a round of all the living-wagons and cadging half a dozen breakfasts, doing his gymnastics in the straw as soon as the horse-tent was up, sleeping, eating again, taking a stroll to see what sort of place they had come to, and then it was time for the afternoon show. Sometimes he strolled into the big tent and watched the strange happenings there (he could make neither head nor tail of them at all), and once he sauntered into the ring and joined the clowns' act, but when they wanted him to do the same thing at the next show he flatly refused and departed to sulk with Zulu.

The people were allowed to see the animals after the show and they all gazed admiringly at Zulu and partner. Once someone tried to be funny and asked why Chequers wasn't in the menagerie tent, and Finnegan scathingly replied that he was on the staff.

The summer passed and life went smoothly. Never had Zulu caused less trouble, and Chequers was everybody's favourite.

One day when Finnegan felt energetic he borrowed some gold paint and neatly printed "& Harlequin" under Zulu's name on his black varnished board—as Chequers never came when he was called unless he wanted to, it didn't matter to him what his name was. Just as Finnegan was running an admiring eye over his handiwork, Dan came into the tent, and when he saw the addition he chuckled approvingly.

"Well, Harlequin, old chap," he said, tickling Chequers under the chin. "You're certainly earning your keep!"

Finnegan grinned. "Faith," he said, "it's that busy he is entirely, what with visiting all his friends an' soft sawdrin' Zulu an' sittin' up here on show, that he'll be wantin' an assistant before we know where we are!"

Chequers just blinked, looking rather sphinx-like, and departed silently. He didn't go off hunting, it was daylight still, anyway, and he headed towards the houses of the little town. They had been three days at this pitch, and Chequers hadn't been wasting his time. He trotted straight to a dip in a garden wall, scrambled up it, walked along the top, crossed a couple of roofs, and dropped down into a narrow little backyard.

He didn't come back till dark, and when he came padding into the horse-tent he was looking so pleased with himself that Finnegan looked twice at him and wondered what "divilment" he'd been up to—but then Dan poked his head in to tell him to hurry up with Zulu as he was on in a couple of minutes, and he didn't have time to wonder any more.

That night they pulled the tent down, and next morning they moved on to the next pitch. They were all too busy to pay much attention to Chequers, and it wasn't till breakfast-time that the bombshell broke.

Chequers started on his cadging rounds as usual—but he wasn't alone! The whole circus stopped work and stared—for behind him, stepping daintily through the grass on small white-stockinged feet, her tail waving gently, came a little orange cat.

She was very coy, and kept gazing at Chequers out

114

of trusting amber eyes, and she was terrifically anxious to make a good impression with all his friends.

She was very coy, and kept gazing at Chequers out of trusting amber eyes

Chequers was simply swelling with pride. He showed her off to everybody, no matter how busy they were, nudging her with his nose and purring like a steam engine. He solemnly inspected every tit-bit they were offered, turning away disgustedly if he didn't think it was enough for two, and by the time he arrived at the newly erected horse-tent there was quite a procession behind him.

"Hi, Finnegan!" shouted one of the clowns. "Come and look what Santa Claus has brought you!"

Finnegan came, and there was a roar of laughter at the look on his face.

"Begorrah, he heard me!" he gasped.

Everyone agreed that the only name for the orange cat was Columbine, and in a couple of days she had settled down to circus life as if she had been born to it, and she even persuaded Zulu that she wasn't going to take Chequers away from him.

Autumn came, and at last the circus arrived at its winter quarters at a farm on the outskirts of a village. Chequers approved of it and so did Columbine, and they didn't have time to grow bored, because when Dan had an engagement with Zulu and his four liberty horses at an indoor circus for Christmas they went too.

Zulu lowered his head to sniff gently at the straw

In the spring they were on the road again; there were all the old friends to greet and some new ones too, and all the old routine to remember again. And then one day there was great excitement in the horse-tent—Finnegan, grinning all over his face and looking like a dog with two tails, let visitors in one by one, and Chequers stood on guard at the end of Zulu's stall. Zulu himself was arching his neck and pricking his ears and lowering his head to sniff gently at the straw—for there, by the side of the feed-box, was a round nest, and in it, curled up in a bundle of heads and tails and paws, lay four kittens—a black one, a marmalade one, an almost white one, and a piebald.

Then Columbine came scampering in, touching noses hurriedly with Chequers, giving a little purr of reassurance to the anxious Zulu, and trotting across to the nest to untangle the kittens—the piebald one had succeeded in sitting on all the rest.

Chequers looked at the four wriggling bundles of fluff and walked across to the nest. Very gently he nosed at the black-and-white kitten, and then stretched out contentedly on the straw to wash himself.

He had a feeling it was going to be fun when Piebald No. 2 started growing up!

Printed for the Publishers by Jarrold & Sons, Ltd., The Empire Press, Norwich
550.1146

ROGER
CARRUTHERS
TEL. 01 340 6526